THE BIG BOOK OF
MOTHER
GOOSE

THE BIG BOOK OF
MOTHER
GOOSE

Illustrated by Alice Schlesinger

Grosset & Dunlap · Publishers · New York

LITHOGRAPHED IN THE UNITED STATES OF AMERICA.
1974 PRINTING
ISBN: 0-448-04200-2 (Trade Edition)
ISBN: 0-448-03650-9 (Library Edition)

Wee Willie Winkie

Doctor Foster

Wee Willie Winkie runs through
  the town,
Upstairs and downstairs, in his
  nightgown;
Rapping at the window, crying
  through the lock,
"Are the children in their beds?
For now it's eight o'clock."

Doctor Foster
  went to Gloucester,
In a shower of rain;
He stepped in a puddle
  up to his middle,
And never went there again.

Hickory, Dickory, Dock!

Where Are You Going?

Hickory, dickory, dock!
The mouse ran up the clock;
The clock struck one,
The mouse ran down,
Hickory, dickory, dock!

"Where are you going,
    my pretty maid?"
"I'm going a-milking, sir," she said.
"May I go with you,
    my pretty maid?"
"You're kindly welcome, sir," she said.

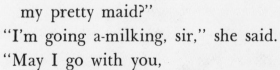

Humpty Dumpty

Humpty Dumpty sat on a wall,
Humpty Dumpty had a great fall;
All the king's horses and all the
   king's men
Couldn't put Humpty Dumpty
   together again.

Little Jack Horner

Little Jack Horner
Sat in the corner,
Eating his Christmas pie;
He put in his thumb,
And pulled out a plum,
And said, "What a good boy am I!"

Mary's Lamb

Mary had a little lamb,
Its fleece was white as snow;
And everywhere that Mary went,
The lamb was sure to go.

Little Polly Flinders

Little Polly Flinders
Sat among the cinders,
Warming her pretty little toes!
Her mother came and caught her,
And whipped her little daughter
For spoiling her nice new clothes.

The Mulberry Bush

Here we go round the mulberry bush,
The mulberry bush, the mulberry bush,
Here we go round the mulberry bush,
On a cold and frosty morning.

This is the way we wash our clothes,
Wash our clothes, wash our clothes,
This is the way we wash our clothes,
On a cold and frosty morning.

      This is the way we iron our clothes,
      Iron our clothes, iron our clothes,
      This is the way we iron our clothes,
      On a cold and frosty morning.

This is the way we sweep our rooms,
Sweep our rooms, sweep our rooms,
This is the way we sweep our rooms,
On a cold and frosty morning.

      This is the way we mend our clothes,
      Mend our clothes, mend our clothes,
      This is the way we mend our clothes,
      On a cold and frosty morning.

This is the way we scrub our floor,
Scrub our floor, scrub our floor,
This is the way we scrub our floor,
On a cold and frosty morning.

      This is the way we bake our bread,
      Bake our bread, bake our bread,
      This is the way we bake our bread,
      On a cold and frosty morning.

It's raining! It's pouring!
The old man is snoring.

Rain, Rain

Rain, rain, go away,
Come again another day;
Little Johnny wants to play.

Rain before seven,
Clear before eleven.

Jumping Joan

Here am I,
Little jumping Joan;
When nobody's with me,
I'm always alone.

Betty Blue

Little Betty Blue
Lost her holiday shoe.
What shall little Betty do?
Give her another
To match the other,
And then she'll walk in two.

My Maid Mary

My maid Mary, she minds her dairy,
When I go hoeing and mowing each morn.
Merrily run the reel, and the spinning wheel,
Whilst I am singing and mowing my corn.

Tommy Tucker

Little Tommy Tucker
Sings for his supper.
What shall we give him?
Brown bread and butter.
How shall he cut it
Without e'er a knife?
How shall he marry
Without e'er a wife?

Cry Baby

Cry, baby, cry!
Put your finger in your eye,
And tell your mother
it wasn't I.

There Was An Old Woman

There was an old woman who lived in a shoe.
She had so many children, she didn't know what to do.
She gave them some broth, without any bread,
Then whipped them all soundly and sent them to bed.

Jack, Be Nimble

Jack, be nimble,
Jack, be quick,
Jack, jump over the candlestick.

One, Two, Three

1, 2, 3, 4, 5,
I caught a hare alive.
6, 7, 8, 9, 10,
I let her go again.

What Are Little Girls Made Of?

What are little girls made of?
What are little girls made of?
Sugar and spice, and all that's nice;
That's what little girls are made of.

What are little boys made of?
What are little boys made of?
Frogs and snails, and puppy-dogs' tails;
That's what little boys are made of.

Polly, Put The Kettle On

Polly, put the kettle on,
Polly, put the kettle on,
Polly, put the kettle on,
And let's drink tea.

Sukey, take it off again,
Sukey, take it off again,
Sukey, take it off again,
They're all gone away.

The Queen Of Hearts

The Queen of Hearts,
She made some tarts,
All on a summer's day.
The Knave of Hearts,
He stole the tarts,
And took them clean away.

The King of Hearts
Called for the tarts,
And beat the Knave full sore.
The Knave of Hearts
Brought back the tarts,
And vowed he'd steal no more.

A Bunch of Blue Ribbons

Oh dear, what can the matter be?
Oh dear, what can the matter be?
Oh dear, what can the matter be?
Johnny's so long at the fair.

He promised he'd buy me a
bunch of blue ribbons,
He promised he'd buy me a
bunch of blue ribbons,
He promised he'd buy me a
bunch of blue ribbons,
To tie up my bonny brown hair.

Little Bo-Peep

Little Bo-Peep has lost her sheep,
And can't tell where to find them;
Leave them alone, and they'll come home,
And bring their tails behind them.

Little Bo-Peep fell fast asleep,
And dreamt she heard them bleating;
But when she awoke, she found it a joke,
For they were still a-fleeting.

Then up she took her little crook,
Determined for to find them;
She found them indeed, but it made her heart bleed,
For they'd left their tails behind them!

It happened one day, as Bo-Peep did stray
Unto a meadow hard by,
There she espied their tails, side by side,
All hung on a tree to dry.

She heaved a sigh, and wiped her eye,
And ran o'er hill and dale,
And tried what she could, as a shepherdess should,
To tack each sheep to its tail.

The Balloon

"What is the news of the day,
Good neighbor, I pray?"
"They say the balloon
Is gone up to the moon!"

Pussy=Cat, Pussy=Cat

"Pussy-Cat, Pussy-Cat, where have you been?"
"I've been to London to visit the Queen."
"Pussy-Cat, Pussy-Cat, what did you there?"
"I frightened a little mouse under the chair."

A Little Girl With A Curl

There was a little girl
    and she had a little curl,
Right in the middle of her forehead.
When she was good,
    she was very, very good,
But when she was bad,
    she was horrid.

Rub=A=Dub=Dub

Rub-a-dub-dub,
Three men in a tub;
And who do you think they be?
The butcher, the baker,
The candlestick maker;
They all jumped out of a rotten potato,
Turn 'em out knaves all three!

Georgie Porgie

Georgie Porgie, pudding and pie,
Kissed the girls and made them cry.
When the boys came out to play,
Georgie Porgie ran away.

Little Sally Waters

Little Sally Waters, sitting in the sun,
Crying and weeping for a young man.
Rise, Sally, rise, wipe off your eyes;
Fly to the east, fly to the west,
Fly to the one that you love best.

Clap Handies

Clap, clap handies,
Mammie's wee, wee ain;
Clap, clap handies,
Daddie's comin' hame,
Hame to his bonny wee bit laddie;
Clap, clap handies,
My wee, wee ain.

Hot-Cross Buns

Hot-cross buns! Hot-cross buns!
One a penny, two a penny,
Hot-cross buns!
If you have no daughters,
Give them to your sons,
One a penny, two a penny,
Hot-cross buns!

Little Tommy Tittlemouse

Little Tommy Tittlemouse
Lived in a little house;
He caught fishes
In other men's ditches.

Ride A Cockhorse

Ride a cockhorse to Banbury Cross,
To see a fine lady on a white horse.
With rings on her fingers,
And bells on her toes,
She shall have music wherever she goes.

A Dillar, A Dollar

A dillar, a dollar,
A ten o'clock scholar,
What makes you come so soon?
You used to come at ten o'clock,
And now you come at noon.

Mistress Mary,
Quite Contrary

Mistress Mary, quite contrary,

How does your garden grow?

With silver bells and cockle shells

And pretty maids all in a row.

The Seasons

Spring is showery, flowery, bowery;

Summer is hoppy, croppy, poppy;

Autumn is wheezy, sneezy, freezy;

Winter is slippy, drippy, nippy.

Ding, Dong, Bell

Ding, dong, bell,
Pussy's in the well!
Who put her in?
Little Johnny Green.
Who pulled her out?
Little Johnny Stout.
What a naughty boy was that
To try to drown poor Pussy-Cat,
Who never did him any harm,
But killed the mice in his father's barn.

Christmas Is Coming

Christmas is coming, the geese are getting fat,
Please put a penny in the old man's hat;
If you haven't got a penny, a ha'penny will do,
If you haven't got a ha'penny, God bless you.

Hey, Diddle, Diddle

Hey, diddle, diddle!
The cat and the fiddle,
The cow jumped over the moon;
The little dog laughed
To see such sport,
And the dish ran away with the spoon.

Bobby Shaftoe

Bobby Shaftoe's gone to sea,
Silver buckles on his knee;
He'll come back and marry me,
Pretty Bobby Shaftoe!

Bobby Shaftoe's fat and fair,
Combing down his yellow hair;
He's my love forevermore,
Pretty Bobby Shaftoe.

Pease-Porridge

Pease-porridge hot,
    Pease-porridge cold,
Pease-porridge in the pot,
    Nine days old.

Some like it hot,
    Some like it cold,
Some like it in the pot,
    Nine days old.

Old King Cole

Old King Cole was a merry old soul,
And a merry old soul was he.
He called for his pipe, he called for his bowl,
And he called for his fiddlers three.

Every fiddler, he had a fine fiddle,
And a very fine fiddle had he.
Twee, tweedle-dee, tweedle-dee went the fiddlers.
Oh, there's none so rare as can compare
With King Cole and his fiddlers three!

Tom, Tom, The Piper's Son

Tom, Tom, the piper's son,
Stole a pig, and away he run,
The pig was eat, and Tom was beat,
And Tom went crying down the street.

To Market

To market, to market, to buy a fat pig,
Home again, home again, jiggety-jig;
To market, to market, to buy a fat hog,
Home again, home again, jiggety-jog.

This Little Pig

This little pig went to market;
This little pig stayed at home;
This little pig had roast beef;
This little pig had none;
This little pig cried, "Wee, wee, wee!"
All the way home.

Rock-A-Bye, Baby

Rock-a-bye, baby, on the tree top!
When the wind blows, the cradle will rock;
When the bough breaks, the cradle will fall;
Down will come baby, cradle and all.

Little Robin Redbreast

Little Robin Redbreast
Sat upon a rail;
Niddle-naddle went his head,
Wiggle-waggle went his tail.

Lucy Locket

Lucy Locket lost her pocket,
Kitty Fisher found it;
There was not a penny in it,
But a ribbon round it.

The Farmer In The Dell

The farmer in the dell,
The farmer in the dell,
Heigh-ho, the dairy-oh,
The farmer in the dell.

The farmer takes a wife, etc.
The wife takes a child, etc.
The child takes a nurse, etc.
The nurse takes a dog, etc.

The dog takes a cat, etc.
The cat takes a rat, etc.
The rat takes the cheese, etc.
The cheese stands alone, etc.

To Babylon

"How many miles is it to Babylon?"
"Threescore miles and ten."
"Can I get there by candlelight?"
"Yes, and back again.
If your heels are nimble and light,
You may get there by candlelight."

I Had A Little Pony

I had a little pony,
His name was Dapple-Gray;
I lent him to a lady
To ride a mile away.

She whipped him, she slashed him,
She rode him through the mire;
I would not lend my pony now
For all the lady's hire.

Sing A Song Of Sixpence

Sing a song of sixpence,
A pocket full of rye;
Four-and-twenty blackbirds
Baked in a pie!

When the pie was opened
The birds began to sing;
Wasn't that a dainty dish
To set before the king?

The king was in the counting-house,
Counting out his money;
The queen was in the parlor,
Eating bread and honey.

The maid was in the garden,
Hanging out the clothes;
When down came a blackbird
And snapped off her nose.

Diddle, Diddle, Dumpling

Diddle, diddle, dumpling, my son John
Went to bed with his breeches on;
One shoe off, and one shoe on;
Diddle, diddle, dumpling, my son John.

Hickety, Pickety

Hickety, pickety, my black hen,
She lays eggs for gentlemen;
Gentlemen come every day
To see what my black hen doth lay.

Curly-Locks

Curly-locks! Curly-locks! Wilt thou be mine?
Thou shalt not wash dishes, nor yet feed swine;
But sit on a cushion, and sew a fine seam
And feed upon strawberries, sugar, and cream!

Old Mother Hubbard

Old Mother Hubbard
Went to the cupboard,
To get her poor dog a bone;
But when she came there,
The cupboard was bare,
And so the poor dog
had none.

Little Boy Blue

Little Boy Blue, come blow your horn!
The sheep's in the meadow, the cow's
   in the corn.
Where is the little boy who looks
   after the sheep?
He's under the haystack, fast asleep.
Will you wake him? No, not I!
For if I do, he's sure to cry.

Bye, Baby Bunting

Bye, baby bunting,
Daddy's gone a-hunting,
To get a little rabbit skin
To wrap the baby bunting in.

Boy And Girl

There was a little boy and a little girl,
Lived in an alley;
Says the little boy to the little girl,
"Shall I, oh, shall I?"

Says the little girl to the little boy.
"What shall we do?"
Says the little boy to the little girl,
"I will kiss you."

Jack And Jill

Jack and Jill went up the hill
To fetch a pail of water;
Jack fell down, and broke his crown,
And Jill came tumbling after.

Up Jack got, and home did trot
As fast as he could caper.
Went to bed to mend his head
With vinegar and brown paper.

Jill came in, and she did grin
To see his paper plaster;
Mother, vexed, did whip her next
For causing Jack's disaster.

Peter, Peter

Peter, Peter, pumpkin-eater,
Had a wife and couldn't keep her;
He put her in a pumpkin shell,
And there he kept her very well.

Ba=a, Ba=a, Black Sheep

Ba-a, ba-a, black sheep, have you any wool?
Yes, sir, yes, sir—three bags full;
One for my master, one for my dame,
And one for the little boy who lives in our lane.

A Sunshiny Shower

A sunshiny shower
Won't last half an hour.

Twinkle, Twinkle

Twinkle, twinkle, little star,
How I wonder what you are!
Up above the world so high,
Like a diamond in the sky.

Wish On A Star

Starlight, star bright,
First star I see tonight.
I wish I may, I wish I might,
Have the wish I wish tonight.

One, He Loves

One, he loves; two, he loves;
Three, he loves, they say;
Four, he loves with all his heart;
Five, he casts away.
Six, he loves; seven, she loves;
Eight, they both love.
Nine, he comes; ten, he tarries;
Eleven, he courts; twelve, he marries.

Tommy Snooks

As Tommy Snooks and Bessy Brooks
Were walking out one Sunday,
Says Tommy Snooks to Bessy Brooks,
"Tomorrow will be Monday."

Prayer

There are four corners on my bed.
There are four angels at its head.
Matthew, Mark, Luke and John,
Bless the bed that I lay on.

To Bed! To Bed!

"To bed! To bed!"
Says Sleepy-head.
"Let's stay awhile," says Slow;
"Put on the pan,"
Says greedy Nan,
"Let's sup before we go."

Little Miss Muffet

Little Miss Muffet sat on a tuffet,
Eating her curds and whey;
There came a big spider,
Who sat down beside her,
And frightened Miss Muffet away!

Pippen Hill

As I was going up Pippen Hill,
Pippen Hill was dirty;
There I met a pretty miss,
And she dropt me a curtsy.

"Little miss, pretty miss,
Blessings light upon you!
If I had half-a-crown a day,
I'd spend it all upon you."

The Months

January

January brings the snow,
Makes our feet and fingers glow.

February

February brings the rain,
Thaws the frozen lake again.

March

March brings breezes loud and shrill,
Stirs the dancing daffodil.

April

April brings the primrose sweet,
Scatters daisies at our feet.

May

May brings flocks of pretty lambs,
Skipping by their fleecy dams.

June

June brings tulips, lilies, roses,
Fills the children's hands with posies.

July

Hot July brings cooling showers,
Apricots and gillyflowers.

August

August brings the sheaves of corn,
Then the harvest home is borne.

September

Warm September brings the fruit,
Sportsmen then begin to shoot.

October

Fresh October brings the pheasant,
Then to gather nuts is pleasant.

November

Dull November brings the blast,
Then the leaves are whirling fast.

December

Chill December brings the sleet,
Blazing fire and Christmas treat.